Mum's Robot

Written by Jill Atkins
Illustrated by
Eleftheria-Garyfallia Leftheri

WAYLAND

M Jm's Robot

First published in 2009
by Wayland

This paperback edition published in 2010 by Wayland

Text copyright © Jill Atkins
Illustration copyright © Eleftheria-Garyfallia Leftheri

Wayland
338 Euston Road
London NW1 3BH

Wayland Australia
Hachette Children's Books
Level 17/207 Kent Street
Sydney, NSW 2000

Series Editor: Louise John
Editor: Katie Powell
Cover design: Paul Cherrill
Design: D.R.ink
Consultant: Shirley Bickler

A CIP catalogue record for this book is available from the British Library.

ISBN 9780750258029 (hbk)
ISBN 9780750259552 (pbk)

Printed in China

Wayland is a division of Hachette Children's Books,
an Hachette UK Company
www.hachette.co.uk

Mum was doing the housework.
"I hate housework," she said.
"Come and help me, Charlie and
Bella. Then you can have your
pocket money."

So, Bella washed up the dishes and Charlie put them away.

"Mum needs a robot to do the housework," said Charlie.

"What a great idea," said Bella. "Let's ask Mad Uncle Albert to make one."

7

They went to Uncle Albert's house.
"Uncle Albert," they called.
"Will you make us a robot?"

Uncle Albert took them to the rubbish tip...

...and the scrap yard.

Then, he took them to the junk shop.
They got everything they needed.

At home, Charlie and Bella made
a list of jobs for the robot.

"This will be easy!" said
Uncle Albert.

Uncle Albert went into the shed and began to work. Bella and Charlie waited outside.

At last, the shed door opened and out clanked the robot.

"Wow!" said Bella. "It's brilliant!"
"Let's try it out," said Charlie.

Mum turned the control. Ding!

The robot went into the kitchen.
Splash! It made too many bubbles.

Crash! It smashed cups and plates.
"This is fun!" laughed Bella.

"Stop!" shouted Dad.

Mum turned the control again. Ding! The robot began to polish the table.

Then, it polished Charlie and Bella.
"Help!" they shouted.

"Stop!" shouted Dad.

Mum turned the control again. Ding!
The robot hoovered the living room.

It looked very nice and tidy.
But then it hoovered up Bella's
homework, Dad's slippers and
Charlie's car.

"Oh, no! It's going to hoover up Fluffy," cried Bella.

"Stop!" said Dad.

Fluffy jumped into Mum's arms just in time.

"Albert!" said Mum. "The robot has got to go."

"We think it's great," laughed Charlie and Bella.

Mum sank into a chair.
"I need a cup of tea," she said.

Suddenly, the robot's control turned by itself. Ding!

"It's going to make some tea," said Bella.

"Oh, no!" said Mum.
"Not more mess!"

The robot made the tea and gave
it to Mum.

"It's a good cup of tea," she said.

"It can make all sorts of drinks," said Mad Uncle Albert.

"Please, Mum, can the robot stay?" asked Charlie and Bella.

"All right," laughed Mum. "Just to make drinks. And only if you three clean up this mess!"